Stationary Objects
A Science Fiction Short Story
Robert J. McCarter

Little Hummingbird Publishing

Contents

Stationary Objects

Oddly, the bridge of Ceres Station always reminded me of my grandmother's simple wood and mud hogan on the Navajo reservation in Arizona.

The room, a large one for the space station, was about six meters across with a cluster of eight workstations in the center of the space, all with low privacy walls.

My grandmother's hogan was eight sided, the door facing the east to welcome the rising sun and good fortune. No electricity. No plumbing. The heat oppressive in the summer. Visiting my grandmother had been like going back in time.

In contrast, stepping on the bridge, my bridge, was like living some kind of sci-fi future. Stepping from the dusty, dry air of the reservation into the sterile, recycled air of Ceres Station. From the gravity of Earth to the artificial gravity of the spinning wheel of the station. From a simple but difficult life rooted in the past, to a modern but difficult life pointed at the future.

Ceres Station orbited the dwarf planet Ceres in the asteroid belt between Mars and Jupiter. We were a long way from home, a long way from my ancestors.

And that moment there, on the threshold of the bridge, seeing the modern cluster of eight workstations and remembering the modest eight-sided home of my ancestors, said a lot about me.

I had embraced the life of science, the life of the future, and left the past and one half of my lineage behind. But I remembered it fondly.

"Captain on the bridge," Lieutenant Simons said loudly, standing and saluting me. The tall Pleiadean was my security officer, he had long blond hair pulled into a tight ponytail—not at all common in space—and elegant androgynous features. He wore the same simple grey jumpsuit we all did with two blue pips on his shoulder marking his rank.

I was hoping for a moment more to just look, to just reflect, before my day at the workstation started.

The twentieth century would be rather disappointed in us, I think. As captain, I spent my day at a workstation processing my queue just like all the other bridge officers. No central throne from which I can bark orders against blaring emergency sirens.

I always liked that moment in the threshold. While I've left my grandmother's ways behind, her legends and her rituals, that small remembrance of her is something I cherished.

I remember the look of her old brown eyes in her deeply wrinkled face the last time I saw her, when I said goodbye to her before leaving Earth. She took my hand in her surprisingly warm hands and said, "Do not forget us down here, Little Mouse, don't forget your ancestors."

She called me "Little Mouse" because my head was always buried in a book, usually some kind of science book my grandfather had given me, and because mice tend to be so detail oriented and near sighted.

The other seven officers on the bridge stood and saluted. I saluted them back. "At ease," I said.

Thoughts of my grandmother lingered. I had been dreaming of her, my blaring alarm taking a long time to pull me out of it this morning. In my dream I was remembering. I had been very young, maybe four, and the yipping of coyotes in the desert had frightened me badly.

My father was a professor and my mother an artist, both in demand. I tend to think that I was an accident, and while my parents were loving, they shipped me off to either my grandmother's hogan in Arizona or my grandfather's cabin in Nova Scotia whenever they could.

"Will they eat me?" I asked my grandmother. This was one of my first times alone with her—the desert and my grandmother were so foreign to me.

She chuckled, it was a dry wispy thing that seemed to go with the desert around us. "No, Little Mouse. They will not eat you. Although you should take care. The coyote is a trickster and can change his form and he will try to fool a little girl like you."

"Why?" I asked.

"Because he is coyote and that is what they do," she said. Not the answer of the scientist side of my family, but very much my grandmother.

I took a deep breath of the recycled air of the space station and shook it off. It was another day and there is always a lot to do on Ceres Station.

———

BEING THE CAPTAIN OF a space station in the asteroid belt can be boring, but it's this special kind of boring. One where you know the mundane can pivot to life threatening in a blink and if you get bored enough you actually hope for it.

On the bridge, I worked my queue, opening up requests, evaluating, replying. I had meetings in my nearby office, a small room just big enough for the table and chairs. It has a large viewscreen on the wall that shows a view of the station, the wheel of it spinning around the long stationary axle, the dark void of space behind it, and the bright round mass of Ceres to the right. The comings and goings of ships are tracked on it.

I like that display. It helps remind me that I am out here in space, not just a worker drone on Earth. But I don't like the meetings, they are generally about personnel issues, or the occasional argument amongst my senior staff on how we should approach a particular problem.

I went to school and studied biology and then xenobiology. I started here working as an alien liaison and then working my way up the ranks. Many days at my workstation, I regretted getting on the command track, trading the mystery of the aliens for the mundanity of command.

But I am well suited to it—except for the occasional boredom—and it is my duty.

The bridge is generally quiet as we all work our eternally filling queues, taking care of task after task. My tasks queued up for me by my officers. Command likes it this way. They can track our efficiency, there is a trail of decisions, it is easy to tell if protocol is followed.

But it felt like it was lacking something, especially today after the dream of my grandmother and her old ways. Honoring your ancestors and the directions. Thinking of animals as more than sources of food or inconveniences you just had to deal with. Embracing the mystery in our lives.

Science knows of mystery and it attacks each and every one of them, desperate to reveal its secrets to make it known.

I am a scientist and this is how I've lived my life, but for my grandmother, mystery was a thing unto itself. Something you respected and allowed.

Mystery was allowed to remain private.

In 2034, at the apogee of social media, when billions were connected, where every person with a phone had a dataset for sale that governments and corporations paid for in ways that were growing more and more authoritarian, the world actually did something about it.

After enough scandals made it clear what was happening, the EU took decisive action and it spread rapidly. Privacy as a basic human right. Control over your own dataset, your digital doppelganger. It could no longer be weaponized against you.

This was right before first contact, before the Pleiadeans changed everything, the world came together and made privacy a basic human right and rebuilt our technology infrastructure in a privacy-first manner.

My bridge and everything about this station reflects that. The eight workstations all face each other in the center of the room. There are privacy walls that block the view of your fellow's workstation.

It can make my job hard, all of our jobs hard, but the feeling was—and still is—that it lets us be fallible, be human, privately. It is built on the belief that being fully human requires privacy and that the costs of privacy are much less than the cost of a society where everything is known.

From my workstation that morning, I stifled a yawn, after reviewing a young ensign's first performance report. He was an apprentice down in the water processing plant, monitoring the purification of water mined on the dwarf planet Ceres. His superior had recommended promoting him onto the crew that managed the much trickier electrolysis process where the water was cracked and turned into oxygen and hydrogen to fuel our ships.

My thoughts kept going back to my grandmother, and the mystery. My metrics were going to be terrible today. Even though my private life was private, my work was measured ruthlessly.

"Captain Allen, we've got another shifter," Simon's voice said in my head. The young lieutenant worked security and was two workstations over, he could have spoken to me directly or put an urgent request into my queue, but he had instead chosen to communicate through my cochlear implant.

My heart started racing and I was fully away. I took a deep breath of the stale air and ran my hand through my short black hair—long gone were the braids of my Navajo heritage in deference to zero-g and how hard long hair can be to manage in space.

"Simons," I said aloud, "will you join me in my office?" I rose from my workstation and stretched.

Ceres Station is a waypoint in our solar system. Ceres is mined for ice, the asteroid belt around us for minerals, and ships coming to or leaving the system almost always stop here.

We are only two day's burn away from our closest entry point into the Fabric, the mysterious network of stable wormholes that make the vast universe a little bit smaller and a whole lot more complicated.

Simons rose crisply, awkwardly unfolding his long limbs from behind the workstation made for humans much shorter than the Pleiadian. Except for his seven-foot-two height, he looked human enough with pale skin and long blond hair.

I felt a stab in my gut after my dream and self-conscious of my short hair. While much of the station is a large rotating wheel that creates inertial force that mimics gravity, we all end up in low or zero-g pretty often and long hair can be difficult to manage. But today, with my dream still present, I realized that a tight braid like my grandmother had made would work. I had cut off part of my heritage for no good reason.

I hadn't thought of my grandmother in years and the dream of her was still with me. I could almost hear her old wispy voice that seemed to carry the weight of our ancient heritage. I could almost feel her rough hands and see her old brown eyes almost disappearing in the deep wrinkles of her face.

She would not approve of my short hair.

"Ma'am?" Simons asked, staring at me. I shook it off and signaled for him to follow me.

Simons was not a man, nor a woman. The Pleiadians have three genders, male and female, of course, and a third that is lacking full reproductive organs. Terrans and Pleiadians come from the same genetic stock but they modified themselves for a third gender, wanting to experience an existence without reproduction at its root.

Simon's look was androgynous, he was thin with elegant cheekbones and full lips. "He" was his chosen pronoun. I'm not sure whether he found our non-binary pronouns inadequate because they didn't quite represent him or he just thought male pronouns suited him better. Given our strict view of privacy and my position as his captain, it was personal, not a question I could ask.

We entered my office, a short walk from the bridge down the central corridor of the station, the Pleiadian following silently. The other six officers on the bridge noticed but didn't think much of it. Their workstations all demanded a lot of attention, each with their own queue of work to be done.

It wasn't so much the basic functioning of the station, its systems could do that by and large on their own, but more the human and social interactions of the 150 souls that called the station home and the fifty or so souls that were here temporarily.

I felt that weight, all those souls, as captain.

Most of us were humans, there were a few Pleiadeans working here, a group on their way to Earth from Arcturus, and our first visitors from Proxima Centauri on extended stay as they learned about our culture.

Souls is the noun we had chosen to use instead of "humans" or "people." They were sentient creatures, but they weren't quite like us.

"Show me," I said to Simons when the door to my small office was closed. It was what a planet-bound person would consider a large closet, but up here, this level of privacy was a luxury.

The room was just big enough for the narrow table and six chairs. One of the long walls of the room was that display I described before of the station, shot from a satellite, with Ceres in view. I could see that the Arcturuns were scheduled to leave tomorrow and a ship from the Pleiades had arrived a few hours ago.

The other long wall was a workstation.

Simons strode over, placed his palm to the large screen to unlock it and started gesturing in front of it.

"Ensign Reynolds," he said, pointing to the image of a woman in the flat grey jumpsuit we all wore, walking down one of the station's corridors. The gentle curve of it under her feet was clear, making it obvious she was in the outer ring.

Her blond hair was about two inches long, she had a hawkish nose and a compact, athletic body discernible under the lumpy form of the jumpsuit. Human and most definitely female. "This is at 08:11 in quadrant L near the hydroponic gardens," Simons said.

The Pleiadian has a thick accent, all the s's drawn out z's, the r's something of a trill with words said individually making his sentences sound stilted. His subvocalized comms were easier to understand, but asking him to do that would be plain rude.

I could speak Pleiadian, but he was much better at English than I was at his language, and this wasn't the time.

"And here she is in quadrant A at 08:20," he said, his long elegant finger pointing towards another image on the screen. This image wasn't clear, showing the back of a woman with blond hair and an athletic build, but it looked like her. She was nearing one of the spokes of the station that led to the central axle the wheel rotated around.

I did the math in my head. Nine minutes to get from one side of the station to the other... it was possible, but you'd have to run and you'd work up a sweat and you'd be seen by other cameras unless you were trying to avoid them. This was looking like a shifter, as Simon had said.

"Any other images of her?" I asked.

Simon shook his head slightly, a gesture he was just starting to master. "Surveillance is at level green, only the cameras at key junctures are live according to the Earth's privacy treaty of 2034."

I nodded and paced the three steps it took to cross my office and then turned and did the three steps it took to go in the other direction.

"Turn all the cameras on," I said.

"But, Captain," he said, "that will trigger the announcement and the shifter will know."

Ceres Station and the mining operations in the asteroid belt were owned by a consortium of corporations and countries. We were highly regulated. We were constantly scrutinized. Changing surveillance levels, and thus reducing privacy levels without notice, was a major infraction of our regulations.

I had some leeway as captain in situations that threatened the safety of the station. Could a shifter do that? Well, sure. They were never up to any good, but there was no way for me to know. Or what if Reynolds wasn't a shifter but just up to something?

"Noted," I said. "Do it. Turn them all on, but make it quick. Find Reynolds. Find both Reynolds if you can."

I don't flummox easily, but shifters... that's plenty reason to be a little off kilter. Especially for me.

———

THE "SHIFTERS," AS WE call them, are something we started seeing eight months ago. We don't actually know what they are or where they come from or even why they are here.

There is some debate as to whether they are even sentient. It's silly, really, but their ability to change their shapes completely and apparently being able to appear and disappear has made some question whether they are biological. And our understanding of consciousness is that it arises from matter, from biology, from our brains in ways we just don't understand. Can an entity without biology be conscious, be sentient?

Biology doesn't guarantee consciousness, of course, but all the species we've encountered since the Pleiadians came, since we started exploring the universe via the Fabric, have been biological and have had some sort of central nervous system.

The Pleiadians uprooted our human-centric view of the world. Many had hoped and dreamed that we weren't alone, but finding that they weren't when they emerged from the Fabric and made first contact was still a shock to our collective consciousness.

It shocked us enough that we became a more cohesive planet in the face of a large, explorable universe. We let the Pleiadians help us deal with our lingering climate issues. We welcomed them in their desire to create an embassy on Earth. They serve, like Simons does, in our explorations of this suddenly smaller universe.

The Pleiadians are the only race we've encountered so far that are like us, built of the same genetic stock, are what we would call "humanoid," although we have evolved somewhat differently.

Conscious beings have developed differently in different star systems. We are told that "humanoids" are in the minority which makes me believe that the shifters are sentient and are here for a reason.

But I suspect their reasons, just as their apparent abilities, are alien to us.

Because of the dream of my grandmother, the pieces of my heritage that I had walled off started coming back.

I had thought my grandmother and her ways were nothing more than superstition. I gave myself to science and left ancient "superstitions" behind.

But the shifters... they defy our understanding, and the ways my ancestors thought had more room for such mysteries. Maybe the theory of panpsychism is right, that consciousness (in varying degrees) is a fundamental part of matter.

My grandmother would have no trouble believing it. She was born on the Hopi reservation in Arizona and they have legends of the coyote being a shape-shifting trickster. Coyotes thrive in the desert, eating rodents and other small animals, their howls and yips rising into the night, echoing over the barren land.

Animals were important to my ancestors and they had many interactions with the playful coyote.

The shifters seemed like coyote to me, like the stories my grandmother used to tell me, her sun-browned skin deeply wrinkled and eroded just like the land around her.

The shifters came and caused problems and disappeared before we could find them or capture them, just like the coyote in my grandmother's stories.

We had one take the shape of Ensign Walters and make love to the ensign's wife which caused a lot of confusion and almost broke up their marriage. I suspect there are more of these types of encounters, but because of our view on privacy the Walters are the only ones that reported it and only because the incident was interfering with their ability to fulfill their duties.

Another time when I was out in the belt inspecting a mining operation, a shifter assumed my form and approved a party that got half the station drunk and left them nearly unfunctional the next day. There were many reports of crew members acting in uncharacteristic ways the next day and many believe it was a shifter, or multiple shifters, using the crew's inebriation to interact and learn about us.

The last encounter, the shifter had taken the form of one of my officers and had been working the bridge and refused to let a ship dock from Arcturus, causing an incident that took me months to clean up.

There did seem to be something playful and curious in what they were doing, in how they were causing us problems. Annoying but playful and very much the coyote trickster my grandmother used to tell me about. But we had no idea how they got here, what they wanted, or why they came.

They were aliens, they had to be, but what kind of alien could assume a physical form at will? And what would its "mind" be like?

And while Native American blood flows through my veins, I am a modern woman and was raised far away from the Arizona deserts. After holding them back for decades, the legends my grandmother told me were ringing in my head.

AFTER THE LAST TWO shifter incidents, this felt personal. The shifter had impersonated me and then inconvenienced me. And this was my station. I know this station. I know every trick, every shortcut, every place the changing artificial gravity can mess with you.

I grabbed my sidearm, swore him to secrecy, left Simons in my office, and headed towards the hub.

Ceres Station looks like a large rotating wheel on a long, thick axle. The wheel with its artificial gravity caused by the spin is where we live and work most of the time.

The thick axle houses the docks and the thrusters we use to keep us stable in orbit, as well as water processing, our docks and shipyards, supplies, and a few quarters for those that prefer zero-g.

The wheel has six spokes that lead to the axle. These spaces are not wasted. There is storage, some hydroponic areas for plants that tolerate lower gravity, and recreation areas. It's a climb. The corridor is round with metal rings attached vertically that make it a ladder you can climb all around the corridor.

Each spoke has a hatch on either end. I ran to the closest one, got through the hatch, and started climbing.

There are gaps here and there in the ladder rings for hatches that lead into storage or hydroponics or the other areas. So the climb is a dance, picking the right tact so you can climb for a good ways before being interrupted by a bulkhead. You must plan it, knowing gravity will grow less and less as you climb until you near the axle and can use only the rungs to guide your soaring path.

My muscles complained at first when I started the climb, feeling every single kilogram. My role as captain is an administrative one, and while I exercise, as we are all required to do, I am not in the same shape I once was.

"Cameras on," Simons said in my head. He wasn't subvocalizing so his strange speech patterns were intact. "Starting the search for Reynolds. As you know, Captain, because of the privacy treaty of 2034, our systems do not have facial scanning technology and I must do this manually and it—"

"Get on with it," I grunted, having set my comms up to be person-to-person with Simons before I left. "Just tell me when you find her."

I moved quickly up the ladder, shifting to avoid the bulkheads, greeting the few crewmembers I met, and welcoming the lessening of gravity that makes me feel stronger than I really am.

I am glad not to live in zero-g, but I do enjoy it. There you can fly. I know it's floating, it's pushing off and controlling your inertia to get from place to place, but it feels like flying.

As I moved, as my body remembered the dance that I have done so many times, I remembered my grandmother and her stories and the trickster coyote. Or the hushed tones she used when she talked of something much darker, of skinwalkers or *naaldooshii*, which translates literally to "with it, he goes on all fours." They are medicine men who use their power for evil and take on the form of an animal to cause others to suffer.

Perhaps the shifters are more skinwalker than coyote trickster, wearing the skin of humans to cause suffering.

I could almost hear my grandmother's wispy laugh as I sored up the last portion of the spoke, gravity negligible.

The spoke ended in another bulkhead and hatch. I checked the display, making sure that the null area was pressurized.

I spun the wheel on the hatch and shook off the memories of my grandmother and her legends. They were nothing more than humans trying to make sense of a world they didn't understand. I was a woman of science and we had a much better grasp on our world and how it works. Not that there wasn't still mystery left. Like this shifter.

I smiled as I left the spoke and entered the axle. The transition can be a bit tricky, leaving the rotating wheel and entering the stationary axle.

We call it the null area because it is the open space in the axle around which the wheel rotates. The coupling of the wheel to the axle is a tricky one. Not being an engineer, I don't really understand it. Think of a wheel rotating on a thick hollow axle being met by six hollow spokes. The wheel has to keep rotating while the null area keeps sealed against the void of space.

That's why there is a hatch and that is why you check pressure before entering the null area.

When I opened the hatch, I heard her. Laughter, the delighted sound of a child playing. Except the voice was not that of a child but that of a woman.

I floated through the opening and turned and sealed the hatch before even looking. It was protocol. It was that important. The null area loses pressure from time to time, that tricky engineering I was telling you about.

Perched on the metal hatch, I looked into the null area. Five meters directly across from me was a hatch for another spoke. Below, spinning and laughing in the zero-g of the null area was Reynolds, her bleach-blond hair a fuzzy mass around her head.

Since I was on a rotating spoke, all six spoke hatches seemed stationary, relative to me, and the axle was rotating.

The image of her floating there stuck struck me. Metaphorically she was me, captured by the momentum of my life choices and my career, spinning, unable to move. Spending my days trapped in the null area of my daily routine. A stationary object that had lost agency.

The thought almost felt foreign, like it wasn't mine. I shook it off.

"Reynolds," I barked, using my best command voice. "Report."

My own hair had gotten a bit long. I didn't come up here often and it was floating awkwardly around my head, black wisps of it impinging with my vision just a bit.

"I'm glad you came," she said, continuing to giggle like she was drunk. "I am stuck."

And she was. It is very hard to transition from a rotating spoke into the null area. Generally, what you do is push off from the wheel's inner rings and aim for one of the airlocks. It's rare to hit it the first time. I could when I was making this transition several times a day, but that was years ago.

But Reynolds was in the dead center of the null area laughing and gently rotating, far enough away from anything that she couldn't move, couldn't arrest her rotation.

I suspect that if I watched long enough that she would have some kind of small bit of inertia that would eventually move her away from the center. Or baring that, the small amount of gravity from Ceres would pull her away, but it looked like she was stuck there.

I had no idea how she did it. No matter what you do leaving the wheel you will have inertia. In zero-g, with only the friction of the air to slow you down, you will make it to another surface.

"This is fun!" she said. "Why don't you join me, Angela."

"That's Captain Allen to you, Ensign," I said. "Now report."

She laughed again. "Your grandmother was right about you." She said it casually, as if we were cousins or childhood friends. Ensign Laura Reynolds had transferred from operations in the belt to the station only six months ago. I had met her. I had reviewed her performance reports, but I didn't know her and she didn't know me and she certainly didn't know my grandmother.

"Did you find Reynolds?" I subvocalized to Simons.

"One moment... Yes, she is in her quarters, Captain," Simons said in my ear. "I see you found the shifter. Do you want me to send reinforcements?"

"Not here," I subvocalized. "Make the null region read as depressurized so no one else enters from the spokes and send personnel to guard the null region airlocks. Contact engineering and tell them we are conducting a test and they are not needed."

It wasn't protocol, it probably wasn't even wise, but we didn't know what we were dealing with... coyote or skinwalker or something entirely different. I didn't want to risk anyone else.

"What was my grandmother right about?" I asked, watching the shifter spin.

"That you are too serious, too regimented." She laughed and waved her arms and kicked her legs like she was trying to swim through water. "She used to always say, what was it...? 'Little Mouse, you are much too serious, my child. Stop worrying, stop trying to figure everything out and play.'"

So the shifter could read minds. That was what my serious, scientific mind told me. This being could not have known my grandmother. She had read my thoughts as I came up the spoke, so focused they were on my grandmother and her legends.

"I miss her," I said quietly. And I did, but I thought I would play along with the game and see where it led.

"She's not really gone," the shifter said. "No one is really gone." After a pause she spoke again, but in a voice that was deep and wispy with age. She spoke in my grandmother's voice and she spoke in Navajo. "Little Mouse, get your pretty head out of your book and come help me shuck this corn."

My mouth went dry and my heart sped up. The shifter wasn't just skimming my surface thoughts but playing deep in my mind if she could speak Navajo in my grandmother's voice.

What would a mind be like that could do that? That could so effortlessly pull memories from deep in my mind. My heart raced out of fear of what she might do and out of excitement for what she was.

"Why are you here?" I asked, barely keeping my voice steady.

The shifter laughed again. "Why not be here?"

"What do you want?" I asked.

"To spin here and have a conversation with you, Angela Little Mouse."

I was getting frustrated. This felt like a game. If the shifter could reach into my mind enough to pull my grandmother's voice out, she knew what I wanted. "Why me?" I asked.

She was here for me. I had known that, maybe a guess, maybe something deeper, but the incidents with the shifters had seemed to have grown more and more personal. I wasn't asking why me about today, but about these visits, about why involve me in this particular mystery.

She didn't reply until her spin brought her facing me and her blue eyes drilled into mine. Reynolds had blue eyes, I knew that, but the eyes that looked at me were electric blue and seemed to almost glow. They weren't the eyes of a human. And for a moment, and I can't be sure this was real, the shifter seemed to stop spinning. "None of you are ready for what is about to come."

DESPITE BEING A "LITTLE mouse," despite always having my head buried in a book, I have never believed that what science understands encompasses even a fraction of what this universe holds.

If the Pleiadeans didn't prove that, then the Fabric and all the places it leads did.

Humanity is out among the stars, now and every day we encounter things that defy our understanding. Like the strange behavior of black holes or some of the non-carbon-based life forms that we have discovered. Or the essential mystery of the stable wormholes known as the Fabric that were shown to us almost fifty years ago and let us travel among the stars and return to tell the tale.

Even though I turned away from my grandmother's ways and turned toward science, even though I had not thought much about her for years, she and her legends made sure that I was aware that what we think we know was not all there is. The mysticism of my ancestors and their lyrical legends are what sketched out some of that great unknown for me without trying to know it, letting it remain a mystery.

I am no medicine woman and I am no shaman and I haven't used those teachings in ages, but I am a great woman's granddaughter and she tried to prepare me for a life that would embrace the mystery.

Even if that mystery is what appears to be one of my crew members spinning in the null area of Ceres Station in the asteroid belt between Mars and Jupiter.

So I laughed at the shifter. She wasn't telling me anything I didn't already know. Humanity was not ready to be out here. How could it be? Was humanity ever ready for any one of the bold steps it had taken?

I could smell my nervous sweat and stale recycled air that is so different from the earth's air. It lacks the subtlety and life as if it is just about our base survival here, and back home it is so much more than that. Space station air is as different from planetary air as filtered water is from the ocean. It lacks dimension and has lost much of its purpose.

I usually don't think about this or notice it, but after hearing my grand-mother's voice, I longed to smell the dry desert air of the reservation, feel the harsh unforgiving sun on my face, hear her tell one of her stories in her wispy old voice.

I could also hear and feel the grinding of the space station's great wheel as it rotated around the axle. Maybe it was a mistake to try bringing gravity with us. It certainly complicated our existence out here, but we evolved under gravity and our bodies quickly changed without it. And toilets are much more pleasant when there is gravity, and eating too.

My senses were suddenly so alive, more alive than they had been in years. The sights, the sounds, the smells of the station are limited and predictable. I think my mind had edited the monotony out, but this being in front of me was somehow waking them up. Waking me up.

Or was this a side effect of the shifter's dive into my mind to pull out memories, to find the voice of my grandmother?

The shifter joined in my laughter and it sounded tiny in the metallic space.

"I am glad you know how unprepared you are," the shifter said. "It gives me a sliver of hope for your species."

And that was one of the reasons I came up here. Not just Little Mouse wanting to do more than read about things, but to be somewhere where your race or your gender didn't matter as much.

Earth was changing, ever so slowly. The heating atmosphere, rising water levels, and shifting populations had made things worse for a few decades, much worse. But after the first Pleiadeans came, after they introduced us to the Fabric, the world had started to get better, bit by bit. But not like up here.

In space your gender mattered less, your gender identification mattered less, your skin color and sexual orientation mattered less.

I was not in the majority on most of these counts, so space made sense for my curious mind and my adventurous heart.

"Hope is important," I said, drawing my sidearm and pointing at the spinning shifter. "Now I must insist that you tell me why you are here."

She didn't seem to care that I was pointing a gun at her. It wasn't a firearm, that would be foolish with the void of space barely held back by the metal can we lived in. It was a flechette, a needle gun, and would likely do little more than sedate her, but it was all I had and I needed answers.

"I told you," she said with a laugh. "I am here to talk to you, Captain Allen. I am here to try to make you apes a little more prepared."

"Prepared for what?" I let the "apes" comment go. Evolutionary-wise it was correct and more than that, I think it spoke to her view of us.

"For the universe," she said quietly. "You've met—what?—six non-terrestrial species so far... that you can identify? My dear Little Mouse, there are so many more, and you apes must learn to play nice together."

Was this turning into a lecture on the foibles of the human race? We had plenty of them and it often took an existential crisis for us to change, but we were fairly aware of them. Weren't we?

"And what species are you?" I asked.

The shifter laughed, and on her next rotation a smile lit up her round face. "Finally! A good question."

But she didn't answer me.

And I was getting impatient.

"Why don't you come with me and you can tell me all about it," I said, gesturing with my flechette.

"Sorry," she said with another laugh. "I'm stuck."

I looked around the null area. The rotating inner circle of the wheel with the six hatches, the walls of the axle, and the two airlocks. Nothing useful. My only choice was to launch myself at her and use my momentum to carry her out of the middle.

But I wasn't going to do that with her conscious.

And maybe this wasn't me "playing nice," but I fired the gun while she was facing away from me, the dart penetrating her jumpsuit and injecting a sedative into her back just below her left shoulder blade.

But she just laughed. Again. It was getting on my nerves.

Trickster indeed.

"Let's have a race," she said when she faced me again, her electric blue eyes a little too wide. "Let's see if you can catch me before I do something... terrible!"

She cackled and began her swimming motion again, and much to my surprise, she started moving out of the center of the null area.

"Is she human?" I subvocalized to Simons.

"She appears to be," he answered in my ear. "Infrared shows a heart and a circulatory system. Although I can't understand why the dart didn't knock her out or how she is doing... that."

Her progress was slow, but it was progress.

I launched myself at her, the flechette outstretched, and put a couple of more darts in her. A second later, I was in the space she had been occupying, but she wasn't there anymore.

I twisted around and looked, hitting the wall of the axle, my breath whooshing out of me. She wasn't in the null zone at all.

She was gone.

―――――

I HAVE PARTS OF my Navajo maternal grandmother and parts of my German paternal grandfather. He was a scientist, one of those that only believed what science believed. It was his religion, and I will admit, it has often been mine. The science of my grandfather has always been easier to embrace than the mystery of my grandmother.x

I used to spend summers in Nova Scotia with him starting when I was eight. He would let me watch any movie I wanted to, read any book, stay up as late as I wanted, and eat whatever I wanted.

He would also not show me one shred of compassion when I ate myself sick with sweets or stayed up too late and came down with a cold or had nightmares from watching horror movies.

Letting me find my own limits was his form of being nurturing.

I loved him for it as a child, he would almost never say no, not unless he thought whatever it was I had set my mind on put me in immediate physical danger.

He thought little of my Navajo grandmother, sniffed at her herbs when I shared what I had learned about them, when I showed him my sage bundle and offered to smudge his cramped, book-filled house. There was no double-blind study or peer-reviewed paper in a prestigious journal, so there was nothing there. I never bothered to share her legends and stories.

My maternal grandmother was all about faith. My paternal grandfather only had faith in science.

I have faith in science. It has served me very well in my life and my career. I use my grandfather to guide my day-to-day decisions. I want to see numbers. I want to hear facts. I want all available data.

For so long that didn't leave room for my grandmother, for the great mystery she always talked about, for the things that science still doesn't understand.

When the shifter disappeared, I needed my grandmother more than my grandfather.

This creature, this intelligence, defined our scientific understanding and seemed more like a Navajo trickster coyote or skinwalker than like any sentient being we had encountered. I had to use the science I had and yet embrace the mystery of what I didn't understand.

"Where the hell did she go?" I asked, not bothering to subvocalize. I had bounced off the wall of the null area and was floating back through it at a leisurely pace. Looking for the shifter, I had had my back to the wall and hadn't been able to catch a hold.

"She... I..." he mumbled, clearly flummoxed. The Pleiadian was rarely caught flat-footed by events. "She's on the other side of the aft airlock. She.... she just disappeared from the null area and materialized there."

"What kind of species are you?" I mumbled.

I twisted around and got myself pointed in the right direction so I would be able to grab ahold when I came to the next wall.

"She's already past the guard and pulling herself along," Simons continued. "He fired on her too, but it did no good. He is in pursuit."

"Call him off," I said. "Lock down that side of the axle, keep people where they are and track her on the cameras."

"But, Captain," Simons said. "We do not know what kind of threat the shifter presents, surely we should—"

"That is an order, Lieutenant," I barked, grabbing a handhold and pulling myself along the wall of the null area to the airlock. "The shifter wants me. And clear the corridor."

"Yes, ma'am," Simons said.

I was sweating, the smell of it sharp with fear. I worked the airlock, and since things weren't pressurized this was just getting myself through two hatches. Even with the emergency, I took the time to close them. That is life in space—you have to take care of the small things no matter what. Those small things are often the only things that keep you alive.

On the other side, the axle corridor is round like the spoke, but larger, about two meters in diameter, with the same kinds of rungs to pull yourself along. Frequent hatchways lead into other areas of the ship.

"The shifter has reached the water processing plant," Simons said in my ear. "She has paused at the hatch and is looking back down the corridor. I believe she is waiting for you, Captain."

I started pulling myself along and had to smile as I felt the joy of flying. I was a touch nauseous from the transition to zero-g, but it was worth it. A small effort and you can soar. And it needed to be a small effort, if you put a lot of energy into it, if you don't control your trajectory perfectly, you will end up careening out of control and bounding your way down the corridor like a ping-pong ball.

We are here because of Ceres and the ice locked away in the rock below us. Water is essential for our survival. Not just to drink, not just to grow food, but to create fuel. Rocket fuel.

Our water processing takes electricity from solar cells and separates the hydrogen in the water from the oxygen via electrolysis. Some of the oxygen is used for life support, some for rocket fuel, and all of the hydrogen is used for rocket fuel.

It is stored in large tanks at the end of the axle as liquid hydrogen and liquid oxygen. Space, quite conveniently, is just about the perfect temperature for keeping the gasses in liquid form. The trick is keeping the sun off the tanks and shielding them from meteorites.

Warm the liquid gasses and they will expand rapidly... even explosively. Or start the hydrogen burning—it's why we use it for rocket fuel—and the whole station is gone.

And that is where the shifter was headed. The most dangerous place on the station.

But why?

"Is she still waiting?" I asked as I gently flicked the rungs passing under me, trying my best to speed up without losing control. It's a strange thing to watch when done well. It's like you are a fish just skimming the bottom of a flat lake, your arms folded at your side and your hands reaching out to barely flick the rungs as they pass.

My grandfather would remind me that inertia in zero-g is very much not flying. My grandmother would laugh and celebrate and wouldn't quibble at the word used to describe it and just celebrate it.

"Yes," Simons said. "She's spinning in circles again and laughing."

The axle, on both sides of the null area, is segmented with airlocks to contain damage. So my flying fish routine would go on for a while, I would stop to work through the two hatches of the airlock, and move on.

All the bulkheads, hatches, and airlocks were about containing the damage from breeches. If our hydrogen stores went up, there would be no containing it.

My hands were sweating as I got through the third and last airlock and could see to the end of the corridor, and could see the shifter.

Still spinning, she saluted me. It was a sloppy salute that seemed either playful or disrespectful, and then... she disappeared.

MY FLIGHT DOWN THE axle corridor was eerie. Simons had done his job and I didn't see one person. That never happens. Someone is always on duty. Something is always going on. It was like I was a ghost haunting the station.

As I spun the wheel on the hatch into water processing, I saw that my hands were shaking. How could they be shaking and I couldn't feel it?

But after I saw it, then I felt it. This pressure, this sense of doom, this roiling nausea that wasn't about the zero-g. I was dealing with an alien that could materialize and dematerialize, that could read minds. What chance did I have to affect the outcome? And whatever happened, this was all on me. This encounter would define me and my future.

If I had a future.

I took a deep breath and willed my hands to stop shaking. I thought of my grandfather and how we were beyond the knowledge of his beloved science. I could almost hear his voice if I had presented him with this. "That, my dear Angela," he would say, "is just a phenomenon that science has not described yet. It is still understandable if you have the right data. So get the right data, child."

And I could almost hear my grandmother. "The Great Mystery is not yours to solve, my little mouse. You with your science may nibble at the edges, but it is more than even you can eat."

They were both right. This alien was understandable, the Fabric was understandable. Given enough time and the right tools. But there would always be more mystery, more things beyond us. It was the height of human hubris to think we could understand and master it all.

The shifter in the form of Ensign Reynolds was there waiting for me in the large room. There were several workstations on one wall as well as a line of prepped spacesuits clipped to the wall ready to be donned, looking something like ghosts, their forms not properly filled out. Another wall was full of closed cabinets where tools and supplies were stored, and another wall was studded with physical controls and valves.

The walls were flat grey like the rest of the station, but the presence of spacesuits and physical controls set this apart from other areas.

Floating in the air was an unconscious ensign, a young man with a shaved head. This room is never left unattended.

There was a digital readout counting down on the workstation next to a bright red bar and labeled H1.

Below the bar, in large red letters, it said, *Alert! Pressure release valve failure. 48 seconds to tank failure.*

Planet side, hot water heaters are built with pressure release valves. Heating water expands and that can create pressure. A sealed hot water heater can, literally, explode. Not flames, but pressurized water and shards of metal exploding out.

Now imagine the same thing happening with a pressurized tank of the same thing you fuel rockets with.

I ignored the unconscious ensign and the grinning alien and pulled myself to the workstation and hooked my feet under the bar that was on the floor in front of it, so I didn't just float away. I pressed my palm to the surface of the display to unlock it. It recognized me and I started gesturing, drilling into the controls and getting more stats on hydrogen tank one.

"Start moving personnel out of this wing of the axle," I said to Simons, not bothering to subvocalize. "Start with those that have a chance, those near the wheel."

"Yes, ma'am," Simons replied in my ear, his tone even, too even. I should have started evacuations sooner.

"And prepare protocol Bravo-6," I said as my hands kept moving and I dived deeper into the menus.

"Can you repeat?" Simons asked, the barest tremor in his voice.

"Bravo Six," I said, enunciating it clearly. "Arm the explosives and prepare to separate the wheel from the axle."

His hesitation was understandable. My first order was to get people moving into the wheel. My second order was to prepare to fire the explosives that would separate the wheel from the axle at the first airlock.

Which would instantly kill anyone on the other side of that airlock, would cripple the wheel and potentially destabilize its orbit around Ceres, but it was better than doing nothing.

I got to the screen I needed. I saw camera views from outside the axle, the emergency vent of the tank was crushed, as if a meteorite had hit it perfectly, and a sliver of shielding had pulled back letting the sun's rays, weak as they were out this far, start to heat up the tank.

I chewed on my lip as the timer counted down.

32 seconds to tank failure.

The H2 tank was not full so I tapped the screen to open the valve between them and let the pressure equalize, but the valve blinked red and the timer continued to count down.

What were the odds? We had small meteorite strikes that did what... both damaged shielding around the tank and did the perfect bit of damage to put one of the hydrogen tanks at risk. And we had a valve malfunctioning.

15 seconds to tank failure.

Enough of my grandfather, it was time for my grandmother. We were way beyond what my science understood and deep into the mystery. I took a deep breath and turned to meet the alien's electric blue eyes.

"What do you want?" I asked.

The workstation, normally silent, started speaking its warning. *10 seconds to tank failure... 9 seconds to tank failure.*

"You," she said, quite simply.

7 seconds to tank failure.

"Fine," I said. "As long as the station survives, you can have me."

3 seconds to tank failure.

She smiled, and even though Reynolds was about thirty, she suddenly looked like she was a child getting everything she had asked for on Christmas morning.

The workstation stopped talking and I turned and looked at the display, the valve had opened between tanks H1 and H2.

I turned back to the alien... I wasn't thinking of her as a shifter anymore or as a coyote or skinwalker. She was an alien, a powerful one at that. This was first contact and we needed to understand these aliens given how this one nearly destroyed Ceres Station with such ease.

I could almost hear my grandmother laughing at me. At my arrogance to think I could truly understand such a mystery as the one I faced.

"Thank you," I said, turning back to that mystery.

She smiled widely but there was mischief in those blue eyes.

"WHERE ARE WE GOING?" I asked from the pilot's seat of a small exploratory vessel named *Doli*. This ship was christened here under my watch and I got to name it. "Doli" is a Navajo word meaning "blue bird."

While I had tried to push away that branch of my heritage, it had slipped back in from time to time, and now... well, I felt a lot more like that little girl watching the Kachina dances for the first time.

The alien, still wearing Reynolds's face, smiled at me from the copilot's chair, but it wasn't her usual giddy smile. It was measured and compassionate.

"Into the Fabric," she nodded towards the dark, inky space visible out the cockpit window, the bulk of Ceres behind us.

I nodded and finished preflight. The tanks were full, supplies loaded, systems nominal.

I glanced back at Simons who was strapped into the third chair. The shifter had requested he come with us, and he had readily agreed. I don't think that his assignment to the station had been that satisfying to him. It was mostly rote tasks and the Pleiadean must have been bored.

He gave me a small smile, although a big one for him, and a nod. He had been through the Fabric getting here, as part of an exchange program we had with his species, but I had not been into the Fabric before, and my heart did a little summersault.

I was a human rediscovering my love for my grandmother and my love of the mystery. Simons was a genderless alien from another star system. Reynolds—I still have no other name for her—was a powerful shape-shifting alien. If nothing else, this was going to be interesting.

I will not be spending my days at a workstation trying to manage an ever-filling queue of mundane tasks. I will not be an administrator responsible for two hundred souls. I will be a xenobiologist heading out into the unknown with two aliens, one of them who is only nominally biological.

The *Doli* is a small ship with a maximum crew of three. All of our exploratory ships are. Any bigger and they won't be able to survive the Fabric, the small, stable wormholes that have made the universe explorable.

The cockpit has the three chairs, large workstation screens mounted in front of them and manual controls all around, but that was mostly for emergencies. The ships know how to fly themselves and human reflexes are not fast enough for travel through the Fabric.

With a vibration that traveled through the *Doli*, the docking clamps released us from the axle and uncombusted hydrogen was vented to move us slowly away from Ceres Station.

My stomach tightened and my heart fluttered. I was feeling so many emotions.

The part of me that was the captain, that was used to being in charge, was not at all happy. I was in the hands of an alien that could materialize and dematerialize, that could take on any form she (or it) wished, that threatened to destroy Ceres Station, my life's work, just to get my attention.

My grandparents, though, that was another story.

My inner grandfather hoped that I could unravel bits of the mystery that the shifters are, furthering science and understanding a race of sentient beings that are clearly not like us... at all. Perhaps there was something essential about consciousness to be discovered.

My inner grandmother was beside herself. I had never traveled into the Fabric, few had, but there was nothing in this universe that represented the great mystery to her more than the Fabric. Who created it? Where did it come from? What was its purpose?

Grandmother would be satisfied with the questions. Grandfather would want to answer them.

And Little Mouse, the child of both sides of her family, was so excited she wanted to scream.

The main thrusters kicked in, the seat pressing hard against my back, squeezing the air out of my lungs. The entrance into the Fabric was just on the Jupiter side of the asteroid belt. It would take us three days to get there. We didn't talk while the ship accelerated and I stared out into the darkness.

The asteroid belt isn't that dense, not like you would have seen in those old movies. There are nearly a million objects out here, but the area is vast. We track them and have their trajectories modeled, constantly updating them, so it's not like the ride was going to be exciting.

But as the acceleration pressed me down, I watched and played the kind of game I would have as a child, one both my grandparents would have approved of. Was that little flash of light a trick of my eye as it tried to process the darkness, or a distant asteroid?

If I was being more like my grandfather, I would look down at the display and see if what I saw was on the moving map of the area. And if I was being like my grandmother, I would let it be a mystery.

"And what are we going to do in the Fabric?" I asked when the acceleration eased.

The alien gave me a small shrug. "We are going to just be, Little Mouse, and see what happens."

"And this will help prepare us apes for what is coming?" I asked.

She laughed, the sound bright and loud in the small space. She nodded out into the darkness. "We shall see, Little Mouse, we shall see."

I smiled back, happier than I had been in years. I wasn't stationary anymore, or station bound. This was the life I wanted, the one that took me into the great mystery my grandmother taught me about and gave me a shot at understanding it better like my grandfather taught me.

Afterword

In 2019 I asked my readers to fill out a survey that I then used as a prompt for this story. I have done pretty well writing for themed anthologies. They come with limitations that are wonderful for focusing the creative spirit. This is another way to do that, except my readers provided me input on this story.

So, what you just read is an experiment. Something rather old-fashioned mixed with something new. I wanted to invoke the feeling of sitting around a campfire with folks shouting out the kind of story they'd like to hear (that would be the old-fashioned part), mixed with the disconnected nature of the internet using surveys for those doing the shouting and ebooks for the delivery of the story (something new).

A modern version of telling a story where the reader and the writer participate together in the genesis of the tale.

The survey results for this story were:

Setting: Space Station
Antagonist: Shape Shifter
Words Used: dancing, flummox, materialize

For a story that is a close cousin of this one, check out *Last Flight of the Acurus*.

He'll risk everything to save his friend

Adventurous by nature and inspired by man's colonization of the Moon and Mars, Rajesh Wells became a belter, one of the pioneering men and woman living and dying in the asteroid belt.

But when disaster strikes and his ship is disabled, Rajesh finds himself facing his biggest challenge yet. With rescue a long way off and his commander and friend spinning helplessly towards an asteroid and certain death, Rajesh ventures out alone into the dark void to save her.

It will take all his courage, every trick he can come up with, just to survive.

In this taunt novelette of friendship and survival in space, Robert J. McCarter, the author of *Seeing Forever*, takes you to the asteroid belt with a surprising tale of friendship and bravery that will keep you on the edge of your seat.

If you want more sci-fi, check out *Seeing Forever*. There is, I kid you not, some shapeshifting going on in that book, but in a much more grounded way. It's an exploration of love and loss in a post-biological life.

A life worth living?

Paul Cruz is no longer human. He's a Singular, his consciousness technological, no longer biological. He was there at the beginning and helped ensure the survival of all the Singulars.

Free from the limits of flesh and blood, he wanted to live forever, but now that he's lost what he cares about the most, forever is too long, much too long.

After suspending himself for decades he is about to enter a virtual world called "Home" to take one last look around. But Home is not what he expected and what he finds will change everything.

When is forever too long?

"In this quiet but far-reaching thriller, author McCarter explores the essence of what it means to be human... Sci-fi as it should be: engaging, moving, and grand in scope". - Kirkus Review

About the Author

Robert J. McCarter is the author of more than fifteen novels and over one hundred and fifty short stories. He is a regular contributor to *Pulphouse Fiction Magazine* and his short fiction has also appeared in *The Saturday Evening Post*, *Andromeda Spaceways Inflight Magazine*, *Everyday Fiction*, and numerous anthologies.

Robert writes in a variety of genres from contemporary fantasy to science fiction and just about everything in between. His diverse background—including a career in software engineering, growing up on a ranch riding horses, and acting—colors the stories he tells.

He lives in the mountains of Arizona with his amazing wife and his ridiculously adorable dogs.

Find out more at RobertJMcCarter.com

Books by Robert J. McCarter

Short Stores Collections

Life After: Stories of Life, Death, and the Places in Between

Anomalous Readings: Thirteen Curious and Confounding Tales

Creatures Featured: Thirteen Stories of Monsters and other Creatures

Contemporary Musings: Sixteen Contemporary Stories from a Sci-Fi Writer

Finding Time: 12 Meticulously Crafted Time Travel Stories

Selected Novels

Seeing Forever

Where the Past Belongs: An Angelica and Ash Time Travel Adventure

Series

The Woody and June versus the Apocalypse: WoodyAndJune.com

A Ghost's Memoir: ShuffledOff.com

Neutrinoman and Lightningirl: A Love Story: Neutrinoman.com

Carterville Mysteries: CartervilleAz.com

Conner Bright Mysteries: RobertJMcCarter.com/series/ConnerBright

Hollow Earth: RobertJMcCarter.com/series/HollowEarth

For more information, go to RobertJMcCarter.com